Pearl Lady Books
presents

The Feathers and The Wind

Written and Illustrated by *Lady S*

Pearl Lady Books 2024

before reading

Who would know more about the world
-us or God?

Who would know more about the world
-the wind or the feathers?

What represents us in this story
-the feathers or the wind?

What represents God in this story
-the feathers or the wind?

Think along with Smarty Suzy as
you read this story.

Then the wind came along
and said to the three,
"You feathers so lovely!
Your place ought to be
where beauty is honored and loveliness praised.
If you'll trust me this day,
then get off this tree
and I'll carry you off
to just such a place."

The three lovely feathers liked the words of the wind,
so they gave it their trust
and let it carry them off;
up from the branch
and into the world.

Where do they want to get to?

So on and on
they floated away;
over the mountains and rivers and trees,
merrily merrily
trusting the wind.

After some time
they came to a park,
where sweet little children
were playing with leaves;
tossing and catching,
and giggling with glee.

The shiny gold feather did see this and say,
"Look how those sweet children
so love the dry leaves.
Imagine how much
they'll adore us instead.
For are we not prettier
than flimsy dry leaves?"

Will the children honor its beauty and praise its loveliness?

And when the wind heard this
it said to the three,
"You feathers, so lovely!
your place ought to be
where beauty is honored
and loveliness praised.
If you'll trust me this day,
forget the dry leaves
and I'll carry you off
to just such a place."

It excited the children to see such a thing!
And they played with that feather,
though as children would play.

They plucked it.

They stomped it.

They swirled it in mud.

And by the end of the day
they just threw it away.

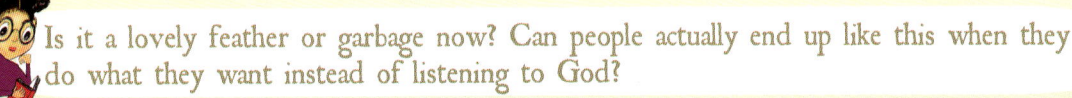
Is it a lovely feather or garbage now? Can people actually end up like this when they do what they want instead of listening to God?

Now the two lovely feathers
liked the words of the wind,
so they gave it their trust
and let it carry them off;
away from the park
and into the world.

So on and on
they floated away;
over the houses with fences and swings,
merrily merrily
trusting the wind.

After some time
they came to a fair,
where hardworking craftsmen
made pillows from plumes;
fluffing and trimming
each plume that they used.

The striking red feather did see this and say,
"Those hardworking craftsmen
so love their white plumes.
Imagine how much
they'll adore us instead.
For are we not prettier
than plain ol' white plumes?"

Will the craftsmen honor its beauty and praise its loveliness?

And when the wind heard this it said to the two,
"You feathers, so lovely!
Your place ought to be
where beauty is honored and loveliness praised.
If you'll trust me this day,
forget the white plumes
and I'll carry you off
to just such a place.

But sadly I tell you,
that red feather strayed.
It abandoned the one
and swooped from the wind,
then flitted on down
to the craftsmen with plumes.

It astonished the craftsmen to see such a thing!
But they cared for that feather,
as they did all their plumes.

They trimmed it.

They fluffed it.

They turned it plain white.

It's not garbage but can we still call it a lovely feather now? What can we call it now?

And now it's shut out of sight
in a pillow they made.

 It's not in the trash but is this the best place for a feather that used to be a lovely feather? Can people who don't listen to God and follow him end up ok but not at their best?

Still the one lovely feather liked the words of the wind, so it gave it its trust and let it carry it off;

far from the fair and into the world.

So on and on
it floated away;
over the signs, the tall buildings, and bridge,
merrily merrily
trusting the wind.

The lovely blue feather did see this and say,
"My goodness! My goodness!
Could that be the queen?
Could it be you've brought me
to be with the queen?
Could I be a feather
that's fit for the queen?"

Will the queen honor its beauty and praise its loveliness?

And when the wind heard this
it said to the one,
"You feather, so lovely! Your place ought to be
where beauty is honored and loveliness praised.
If you'll trust me this day, then hold on to me
and I'll place you down there in the hands of the queen."

Why should it still stick with the wind even when it knows for sure where the wind wants it to be?

So gladly I tell you,
that blue feather stayed.
It clung to a breeze
that swept through the lounge,
then gently it fell
in the queen's waiting hand.

Would it have gently landed in the queen's hand all by itself? Would something else have happened?

It made the queen giddy to have such a gift.

She kissed and caressed it with tender delight.

She ordered Hat-maker to make a new hat displaying that feather to all who can see.

And from then on, through history that feather remains a treasure that sits on a queen's favorite hat!

Can I think of times when I listened to God and things went great for me?

Can I think of times I didn't lsten to God and things went bad for me?

Can I think of times I didn't listen and things didn't go bad but I know things could have been better if I had listened?

The Shiny Gold feather brought temporary joy to children while they played, but had not followed the wind so it had a sad end.

The Striking Red feather too served a purpose of comfort, but it was changed and hidden away when it didnt trust the wind. The Lovely Blue feather, trusted the wind, had the same chances to follow its own path, like the Gold and Red feathers, but persisted and followed the wind.

The Lovely Blue feather was rewarded by the wind, finding a place of prominence and prestige, because it followed the wind to the very end. The blue feather trusted the wind more than its limited understanding of the world. It trusted that its place was not the place of dried leaves or white plumes. It allowed the wind to take it to the place where unlike the other feathers, its beauty was not stripped away, but honored and praised.

Trust in the Lord with all your heart and lean not on your own understanding. In all your ways acknowledge him and he shall direct your path
Proverbs 3:5-6

There is a way that seems right to a man but the end is death.
Proverbs 14:12

You make known to me the path of life; in your presence, there is fullness of joy; at your right hand are pleasures forevermore
Psalm 16:11

Children of God must put their trust in God and let him guide us like feathers in the wind. God knows more about the world than we do. He knows the end of every path we might take, and he knows what path is best for us. He wants us to trust him so he can lead us to the right path (Proverbs 3:5-6).

We can be sure we'll be happy when we trust God to lead us. He says his plans for us are good and will bring us hope and our expected good ending. (Jeremiah 29:11-12).

If we put our trust in ourselves or in others instead of God, we'll be disappointed. But we'll be blessed if we trust God (Jeremiah 17:5-8).

We show that we trust God when we follow the leading of the Holy Spirit (Galatians 5:25) and when we obey the teachings of Christ in the Word of God. Jesus says that those who practice what they learn from the Word of God are sure to be blessed (Luke 11:28).

Do we know these words
Lets do the "Use it in a sentence" challenge.
We can check to see how the words are used in this book

Honored
To be highly respected

Glee
Feeling so much joy or happiness

Flimsy
Easy to break or destroy

Flitted
Move quickly from one place to another

Astonished
Feeling great surprise or amazement

Giddy
When you're so excited you act silly

Caressed
To touch or stroke gently and lovingly

Temporary
Does not last for a long time

Persisted
Continuing even though it's hard

Prominence and Prestige
Being important   Being praiseworthy

Chiamaka signs her artwork as "Lady S" and is a devoted follower of Christ. She has a Masters degree in Philosophy and Education from Teachers College, Columbia University and has worked as a teacher for several years. Lady S produces stories to entertain and prompt children to think creatively & philosophically about important biblical lessons. She believes that stories are a fundamental tool for shaping the character of developing minds. She hopes that her stories can help nurture godly attributes.

Donate to this Children's ministry

$ladystoryteller

Pearl Lady Books llc

Text: 6468674880

Email: pearlladybooks@gmail.com

Follow

   @pearlladybooks

pearllady-s.com

 If you enjoyed this story please let me know by leaving me a review!!!

You can also scan and e-mail me your fan letter

Find out more about Lady S and her books

fan mail

To *Lady S*

From

Trace the path this feather needs to take to get to the queen

Proverbs 14:12 There is a way that seems right to a man but the end is death

Psalm 16:11 Lord you make the path of life known to me ...

Interesting facts

The place in this story is called Pearlland. Queen Magenta is the ruler of Pearlland. She's even on the money! The Pearlland money is called Pearlys.

10 Pearlys can buy you 5 baskets of apples

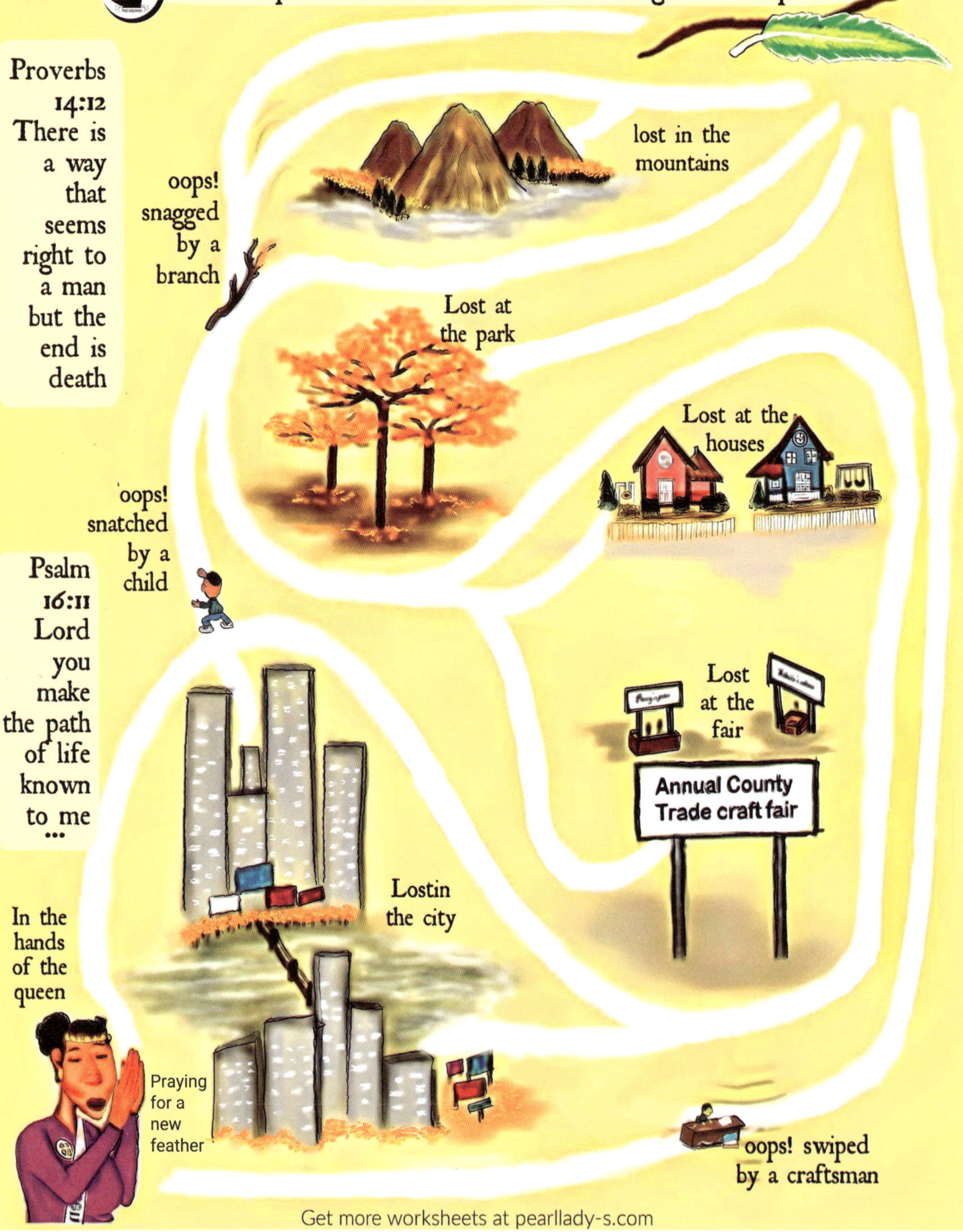

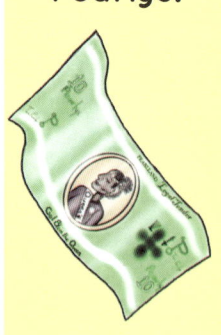